MW00914394

DOMESTIC VIOLENCE

SURVIVOR'S STORIES

BIG BOYS DON'T CRY

KEN BUTLER

Copyright © 2017 Ken Butler
All rights reserved
First Edition

PAGE PUBLISHING, INC.
New York, NY

First originally published by Page Publishing, Inc. 2017

ISBN 978-1-68348-151-5 (Paperback)
ISBN 978-1-68348-152-2 (Digital)

Printed in the United States of America

The meaning of life is hard to discover until
you live a life that has meaning to you.
—Ken Butler

"Hope is always a choice at your own fingertips."

Thank you to my wife, who is my "heart and soul." Love, Honeth

Thank you to our sons, EJ and TY. Finish well, boys, and be the best you can be. Love, Daddio!

Thank you to my family members, close friends, trusted colleagues, teachers, and mentors that encouraged me to write about my journey. With respect, Kenny B.

Thank you to my tae kwon do teacher for seeing the potential in me and providing me with life lessons that go far beyond kicking and punching.

This book is dedicated to all my siblings, who inspired and motivated me to become the man I am today. I have learned so much from everyone in so many different ways. Love, Boo Boo.

1. Gus taught me self-worth.
2. Rosemary taught me how to laugh.
3. Lois taught me how to be a better brother.
4. Butch taught me to never trust anyone 100 percent.
5. Norma taught me how to push myself.
6. Doris taught me how to be calm.
7. David taught me how to never give up.
8. Kenny taught me how to love myself.
9. Robert taught me to stick up for myself.
10. Barbara taught me the power of forgiveness.

This page is dedicated to our wonderful mother.

Just forty-eight hours after this picture was taken, the heavens opened and our mother passed away.

You may not see anything unusual about this picture. A mother with her son. But if you knew our mother she was always strong. Now when I look back at this picture at that moment she was resting her head on my shoulder for the very first time in my life. It was always the other way around. Some folks wish they had one more moment to say good-bye, well I did, and I am so grateful. That picture was taken on a Tuesday and my mother came to my house on a Wednesday. I recall her hug was a little bit tighter, a little bit longer that day.

Mother passed away on Thursday morning, quietly, at the table I gave her, in the chair that I gave her. For many years, I looked at that chair as the chair she died in and now I look at that chair as the chair she lived in. Millions of conversations with kids, grandkids, and great-grandkids, Mother did more than just die in this chair; she fostered generations to be self-inspired.

For me, this chair holds the secret to me being able to write this book. Now I sit proudly in her chair. I am inspired by goodness each and every time I sit in this chair. In fact, nearly all of this book was written while sitting in this chair.

The chair is a metaphor for sure. A good home life needs a strong base, a place for comfort, protection from falling back.

I love this chair.

Elizabeth Chase Butler
June 7, 1921 to June 9, 2011

Contents

Before I begin sharing my personal journey with my life story, I want to point out that the majority of my life has been filled with great friends, great experiences, and most of all a great family. I did, however, have a series of traumatic experiences along the way. I was told by many close friends and family that I should write a book. I have heard there is a book in all of us. Well, my goal is to share my book with you and inspire you to write your book. Some books are filled with lots of words that lead up to the main points. That is not how I live my life and that is not how I wrote my book. The book has a very simple but powerful flow. I write about twenty-five experiences that I feel shaped my character and nudged me in my life path.

My book is in chronological order and begins when I was six years old. While writing the book, I shared the content with my wife and, in some cases, I shared painful memories that I have never told anyone in my entire life, not even my wife.

My life began on November 20, 1961, and I was born in lovely warm San Diego, California. Then we moved back to the state of Rhode Island when I was only six months old.

Pictures can paint one thousand words; memories can paint
a panorama that is hard to remove from your view.

 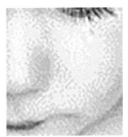

CHAPTER 1

Burning Down the House in Whiskey Land!

Our father would get so intoxicated that he would frequently choose to start fires in our house while we were sleeping. Although he was a master masonry man, he did not always use his well-constructed fireplaces to light the fires. I guess, among other issues, he had an Issue with fire. Many times, mom would take her post on the floor next to the couch where he would finally pass out for the night. Mom would sleep on the floor so our dad would trip over her body and she would be woken up before he could do harm. We all suffered from his dark hand. I intend to talk candidly about what I experienced.

One night, when I was only five years old, I was frightened by loud bangs and yelling. I crawled out from under the twin's crib where my bed was. I stepped out of that room and saw our drunken father choking our mom while holding a knife to her throat. My oldest brother, Gus, woke up and placed himself in the middle of this battle. I remember the yelling and this was terrifying. My other brother, Butch, then pulled my brother and father apart and the fight continued between my brothers and father for several minutes. In the end, my mother and brothers were "fine," well in Butler household terms anyway. We all went back to bed. However, I never fell back to sleep that night and never shared the event with anyone. But to this day, I am up most nights alone in a perpetual anxious state. It is like I avoid going to sleep. After all these years, I am still anxious to close my eyes. Mind you, I have a calm home life, a wonderful wife and two fantastic sons. No guns, no knives, no fires, and no fights. I have broken the cycle externally for my family. However, my internal struggle and terror remains in my own mind. Over and over. Now as I begin writing about my story almost forty-eight years ago and that image simply does not ever go away. In fact, it replays itself over and over. Of course, over the years, I have found ways to keep it less vivid but I am telling you that it is always there.

Reflection

No fighting! As a rule, we should all avoid conflict. If you need to argue, be sure that you do it away from your children. What they see and hear stays with them for the rest of their life. Well, at least, it is that way for me. My experience was extreme but I assure you, each child holds the tears and fears of their home life for a long time. No family is perfect but if you stick to the basics such as respect, keep your hands to yourself, and if you can't say something nice then don't say it at all, you can avoid additional stress and in some cases long-term emotional damage.

Forgiveness works best when it is forever because a simple glance back, just for a moment, forces unnecessary redundant pain.

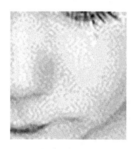

CHAPTER 2

Before the Battles, There Was a War

Walter Butler at his Tavern in East Greenwich circa 1940

Let's take a few steps back in time and gain insights into who this man was before he became our father.

He was a Navy man and earned one silver and two bronze stars while participating in seven major engagements in WWII Pacific War Theatre. Gunners mate, third class. To be sure, I respect and acknowledge my father's service to our country. Our father was fiercely loyal to both parents. My father was one of ten children and my grandfather Walter owned a bar. I suspect that set my father up to enjoy drinking very early.

Here is the story as told by my father to my mother that we now believe lead to my father's alcoholism and what we now know as posttraumatic stress disorder (PTSD) that military men and women

experience while serving in combat situations. War had a terrible psychological impact on his life.

My father left for the service and while out at sea he received a call that his father was ill, so he was granted permission to return stateside to be with his father before he passed away. I know personally that losing a father has a devastating impact and can empathize with his emotions during this time. While dealing with the loss of his father, his mother became ill and she asked him not to go back to sea. Aubrey had made a commitment to the US Navy that could not be broken. As he was ready to leave stateside and report for duty, his mother said, "If you go... I will not be here when you return." Well, my father was fully committed to the US Navy and felt it was not an honorable option not to return. Six months back at sea while serving our great country he was notified that his mother had passed away. Returning home from war without either of his parents was a trigger for depression that, according to our mother, he never recovered from emotionally and the heavy drinking ensued. The drinking caused him to miss his reenlistment date.

This is not a defense for his violent and abusive actions, which I witnessed and experienced. I just feel it is necessary to be respectful of the man he was, before marrying my mom. What he did to my mother and all of his children are unforgettable and inexcusable.

Reflection

Although unforgettable and inexcusable, I learned through my mother, my faith, and my sisters that in order to live beyond the pain one must forgive. However, it is human nature to harbor ill will and

I can confess I spent way too many years harboring ill will towards one monster or the other. Take great care in your approach with the ability to forgive. Buddha, Catholicism, Christianity, all teach forgiveness, and in my opinion, is one of the very best medicines to heal a broken heart, a bruised spirit, or emotional damage.

*"Good friends should be good to you and most
certainly must be good for you."*

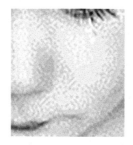

CHAPTER 3

A Sobering Experience

 I have one best friend that has always been my friend. We shared our first beer together, road our first motorcycles together, and we hung out from the time we were fourteen and sixteen until our twenties.

In life you can only hope that you meet and keep friends that are there to guide you, steer you into good things and away from bad things. In fact, my best friend in this world helped me with the final edits in this book.

The power and influence friends can have on you is tremendous and should not be taken lightly. Dave Woodward (AKA) Woody has been there for me even when we lived a thousand miles apart. For that I feel blessed. Physical distance should never hinder true relationships. Time should never dull the connection if the friendship is true. We should all be so blessed to have a friend metamorphose into a positive brother level relationship. As Mrs. Woodward used to say, "Ken, you are Woody's brother from another mother." Forty years later, Woody and I meet weekly to play pool together and we will ride motorcycles again real soon. Only this time it will be a lot slower and with a helmet. My father made horrible choices with his "Friends".

My parents realized alcoholism was taking a toll early in their marriage. Their relationship was not healthy as my father drank heavily all of the time. So after ten years and seven kids, they loaded the station wagon and drove from Rhode Island to California in search of better work, a sober lifestyle, and a new start. It was a pilgrimage to create a better life.

I asked my older sisters to tell me about the time in California. Each sister described a more peaceful time, free of alcohol and abuse. Their lives were looking brighter than ever and hopeful. As far as I could tell through my sisters' discussions, California was normal everyday life. But there was something that was pulling my father back to Rhode Island. So, my parents packed up eight kids this time and drove back across the country to Rhode Island. Yes, I was number eight. I was born in California during what was the best fourteen months of my mother's married life with our father. So off we went traveling across the country going back to Rhode Island. Our dad didn't have a house, job, or plan for the family.

My father was a skilled mason and began his own company. He did really well, made good money, had men working for him, respect in the industry as a solid man who knew how to do brick work. However, he still had the incredible compulsion to drink when he was with his friends. The return to Rhode Island proved too hard for him to remain sober. He began drinking regularly again and when I say drink, it was uncontrollable. He would spend all his week's pay on Friday night and was unable to provide his family with food the next day.

Reflection

Alcohol plays a dynamic role in homes, society, communities, and families. One powerful dynamic is how friends can impact your choices. Peer pressure is real but I would say a friend's influence is much stronger. Pick your friends carefully and explore the fact that "like attracts like." In some cases, one friend can influence your actions that can have devastating outcomes. Forty-five years ago, alcoholism wasn't really discussed but in today's world, the treatment is outstanding and there is hope for those struggling with addiction of all types. I will say this, if you have someone in your life that is struggling with addiction work to stage an intervention because they can work.

"Family genes are always part of your DNA, but some values are instilled and some are repelled."

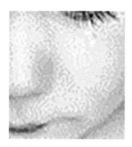

CHAPTER 4

My Genesis

My story illustrates the many challenges along the road of life. I share my experiences and thoughts and hope to inspire others to acknowledge their own story.

I share experiences that are raw and may be upsetting, but all of them have literally forced me in one direction or the other. In my opinion, we only have two things we focus on, regardless of who we are or how much money we have; we seek comfort and work endlessly to avoid pain.

I have spent my entire life doing just that. It's been an exhausting process. Avoiding pain and fearing the truth is like being a fugitive from yourself. Writing this book has allowed me to relax in my own skin for the first time in over forty-six years. My intention is to show that bad things do happen to us all. The key is to create positive emotional attitudes about any given situation.

Reflection

Although it has taken me nearly forty-eight years to value both parents for who they were before giving us life, this newly experienced peaceful time in my mind is fantastic. I did not always agree and certainly did not always benefit from their care but the healing process is very important. No matter what the pain, no matter what the sorrow, no matter what the offense, you must forgive so that you can live with yourself.

"Some say practice is the mother of mastery. I say, preparation comes way before practice and mastery is best obtained with all of the right tools but if you don't have the tools, go with what you got and enjoy the ride."

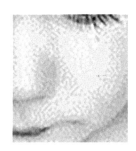

CHAPTER 5

Making Something from Nothing

I am six years old. On this morning, my father asked me to go with him to drop off some trash in his pickup truck. I recall it was very cool and it seemed like a rite of passage to go for a ride with dad. My siblings were making a big deal that it was my turn to go with dad. He dumped off the trash and this broken bike caught my eye. I asked if I could have it and he looked at me with fierce eyes, and we stared at each other for what seemed forever.

He said, "Yes, go get it," so I climbed on the heap of garbage.

As I loaded the bike into the pickup, he said, "What color would you like to paint it?"

I said, "Red."

He said, "How about green, son?"

On the way out of the dump, we stopped at the "dump shack" where a man was sitting, drinking beer, and guarding the trash I guess. My father knew the trash guard and spoke to him from the truck. They shared a morning beer.

My father asked the trash guard, "Got any more of that leftover green paint?"

The man said yes and the man gave my father half a can of evergreen paint, you know the deep green used for parks.

The guy said, "It is park green."

We went home and my dad gave me a six-inch house paintbrush and said, "If you want to paint your new bike, here you go."

I began to paint that bike. Of course, I had no idea of the required preparation or direction from anyone that you can't just paint rusty metal. So, I pressed on and painted that bike. I was so proud of that bike and as I rode down the street, I still recall the pride I felt. I soon after noticed the paint simply rolling off the bike onto the road.

Reflection

That day, I learned that if you want something you need to go get it even when it's an old bike on a pile of trash.

I never imagined how much the green bike lessons would pay off so many ways in my life. I can say that learning how to get by with whatever you have can give you the chance to be creative. Being poor absolutely inspires you to relentlessly find ways to make things work. I think about my green bike day all the time and I intertwine the lesson into almost everything I do. Although my time around my father was very brief, the bike lesson is recharged over and over.

"One discouraging word can last a lifetime; one encouraging word can change a life."

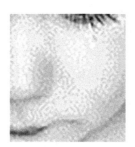

CHAPTER 6

Big Boys Don't Cry

Losing my father when I was only six years old changed my life… forever. It was April and everything was coming together just as planned, the sun was out, the Easter bunny was coming. But my parents were apart. The night before Easter Sunday, my father came from the apartment he was staying at while my parents were separated. This happened very often due to my father's increased violence and abuse. He came in our house to drop off three gray suits. One for David, one for Bobby, and one for me. For some reason, I got caught in the stairway trying to get to my mom. My father stopped me on my way down. He began to tease me and I began to cry. Now I know why no one came to see what the matter was and that is because our entire house was in fear. He was pushing me and saying "big boys don't cry" and "don't be a baby." He said boys don't cry and he kept pushing me and teasing me. Not hard pushes that hurt on impact but more like bullying/embarrassing pushes that bruise your soul. He just kept teasing me and no one in the house either heard me or wanted to get in the middle. After all, it was the eve of Easter Sunday and my mother worked so hard to create an environment of peace. My father brought us the little gray suits and we were all set for Easter Sunday and then church. The more of that little gray suit I put on the prouder I became and, yes, I can recall smiling big that morning. We went to church and mind you, my father was nowhere to be found in the pews. We pulled up to our house after church and I recall what seemed like hundreds of cars and hundreds of people in our yard. Now in retrospect it was most likely family members and a few remaining "friends" as I am unsure by that time if he actually had any friends that he did not owe money to or that owed him money.

Everyone was soon crying and I kept asking "what was the matter" to everyone. Finally, my older brother Dave said, "Dad is dead," and then David literally stuck his head into a hole in the ground and screamed so loud that it must have been heard all the way to hell and back. I am certain my brother David, age eight at the time, never recovered and later in the book you will learn how strong-willed David was. I wanted to cry but the very last thing my Dad said was "Big boys Don't cry." That was the beginning of a long stretch of not crying.

Reflection

Be very careful what you say to children. My advice, if you said anything that you wish you could take back, go back and say you're sorry and explain why you are wrong, especially to a child. Don't let a negative legacy get rooted in your children's mind. There is an old saying that says, "You can't un-ring a bell." Not true exactly. Even children appreciate apologies and once that is done, you can build stronger, more valuable memories. Today I still have a difficult time crying but I have learned how to express myself very well through art and writing. Our father no doubt became a very bad man and I can only hope that other mean dads learn to be careful with their words and actions. I am not a perfect father but I have broken the cycle of domestic violence.

"It is often pondered; if we could live our life again what would we do differently? For me, I would be stronger sooner for my siblings."

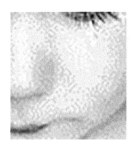

CHAPTER 7

Ashes to Ashes and Dust to Gus

At my father's gravesite was the first of only two times in my life I saw our mother with her head down. She had ten children to raise and she did a fabulous job! You could tell we were all in a state of shock. Sort of a rag tag bunch, all completely lost. Our father was the breadwinner. But my big brother Gus stood there boldly. Can you imagine the load on a young man's shoulders when at age twenty-one you become the man of the house? My brother Gus taught me to stand there boldly. He also died way too young. I can't imagine the burden on my mother. When my wife leaves on business for two days, my sons treat me like a substitute teacher. We go from having cheerios for breakfast to having SpaghettiOs for breakfast very quickly. The heaviness being a single parent to ten children must have been so stressful at that very moment. This was the first time I saw my mother with her head down. Of course, big brother Gus now had to lead the way at age twenty-one. Think about that for a second. When I was twenty-one, I was driving to Florida with a friend to soak up the sun. Gus was now the man of the house.

I may have lost a father but I had a mother that was stronger than any one I have ever met in my life. She is my hero!

My mother had already lost her first husband in WWII and now she was burying her second husband. So, in essence, my mother lost two husbands to war in one way or the other.

My mother never remarried and one day when I was a grown man I asked her why, and she said, "Why would I want another man? I loved your father."

In writing, I had the painful realization that I had never asked what life was like before the death of our father. It hit me like a ton of bricks that I had never asked this question before and I have seven older siblings that I could ask but I guess I was never ready to hear the answer.

I mean, was our father pure evil in every sense of the word?

Did he have any good qualities? I asked my three oldest sisters the same question, "Was there any time other than our time in California that our home was not filled with violence and abuse?" The answer was "No." When writing this book about my journey I was respectful of my siblings' stories but each one shares a glimpse of what life was like and I have their permission to share.

My oldest sister Rosemary recalls that our father was brutally mean when he was intoxicated and he was the nicest guy when he was sober. She explained that it was chaos every single day. She shared one story with me that was particularly painful to hear and extremely hard for my sister to talk about even after sixty years.

It was winter in New England with snow on the ground and freezing outside. My father was drunk as they called it way before our society softened the term to "intoxicated"

My parents were fighting about his ABUSE. My father literally kicked my mother out of the house and my mother just began walking down the street. Who knows where she was headed, perhaps to a "friend's" house down the street that mother learned later had betrayed her and had an affair with our father. My father sent my oldest sister and my oldest brother out in the snow to get our mother. My sister said, "Dad, we are not dressed and it is winter outside." He simply forced them both out the door and said, "Go get your mother." So my sister and oldest brother ran after our mom and convinced her to come back to the house.

As you can picture in your mind, my mother and two of her small children had to walk back to our house in the freezing cold and knock on the door of their own house.

My father opened the door, grabbed my big sister and brother, then yelled at my mother and said, "I thought I told you to get the hell out of here?" Then he slammed the door in her face and then simply sent the kids to bed. That type of story would be repeated over and over, so I will not continue with that part of our genesis. I choose to focus on what a great family we have and the love and support we shared. Of course, there are stories in the coming chapters that are not positive but I do express how I survived and what I did about the awful things that happened to me.

Reflection

I feel I always knew there were bad stories, and over time I insulated myself through time, distance, and sibling relationships. This particular emotional strategy was done so I did not have to deal with the past beyond my own pain. When you isolate yourself from connections, this can have negative implications on all relationships. Over time, you find ways to avoid deep connections. For me, it was as simple as not remembering names. Not because I did not like someone, it was simply because it kept me from getting close. I am sure there is a medical term but for me it was me keeping my distance to avoid the inevitable hurt or broken trust. Well, now I have many friends at all levels and all healthy and respectful, and yes, I know their names, and my life is much richer because of many friends. My family ties are stronger than ever and this book has brought us together even though we live in different states.

"When life hands you nothing, not even lemons, then you must start a water stand and then build from there."

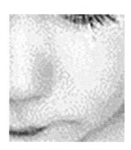

CHAPTER 8

Poor Kenny

Being poor is hard for anyone but, even at age six I realized other kids had it worse than us. Being "poor" is a state of mind. My state of poorness led to creativity and prosperity. It is there, if you try and if you look.

We had very little growing up. If you can imagine at one point my father had fifteen to twenty men working for him in his masonry business. Then you add alcoholism in the early fifties and then the picture changes dramatically.

I reflect on the time in my life from age six to fifty-four and all the obstacles and challenges that I faced along the way, and more importantly, what I experienced. I talk about what I did to survive. In my case, as in almost every case regarding domestic violence, that one must first survive and then they must learn to thrive.

After forty-six years, I am finally in the thriving stage. I am not talking about money. I am talking about finally being comfortable in my own skin and able to talk about the abuses as a matter of fact and not hiding behind a strong appearance.

I was the eighth child. After my father died, I realized almost instantaneously that I would be on my own for most things in life.

For me, it triggered imagination and allowed me to dream and be creative very early. My brothers and I would use our sisters' shoes as cars and our older brothers' work boots as trucks. This gives you an example of how being poor can be an instrument of creativity and can fuel your desire to make your world around you more comfortable.

I have learned by reading many books, it has been written a thousand different ways and that is this: No matter who you are or what your status is in this life, we all basically seek two fundamental things,

I guess it is the base for all living things.

Example: One family seeks comfort in a seven thousand square foot home and others seek comfort under a bridge. To me, the desire to seek comfort is the same. We all get it in different ways.

The millionaire may seek to avoid pain by not losing millions in the stock market, and the person under the bridge seeks to avoid pain from not getting frostbite.

Again, we all avoid pain but we all get there in different ways.

For forty-eight years, I have worked tirelessly to avoid pain and just recently began to feel comfort. I am not talking about financial status. My avoidance of pain morphed into a burning desire to get comfortable.

The picture below on the left, illustrates a gift my younger brother gave me. I was in my thirty's and finally bought my dream car, on the right, a classic 1974 red corvette. Certainly, this car was on the bucket list.

My younger brother Robert wanted to be sure that I never forgot where I came from. This car-shoe my brother made is displayed in my workshop and is one of my prized possessions. No one in my life is stronger than my brother Robert. I have learned to be strong from 'Bert" and admire his ability to always find the good in this world.

Reflection

Embrace what you have and be creative with whatever your circumstances. We have all heard if you are given lemons, then make lemonade. Well for me and many others in this world, even the lemons are not present.

You must look beyond the tangible in order to survive being poor. When the tangibles are not there then you must create out of thin air your dream, and that is where the magic of being poor comes into play.

Even if you are missing the lemons then press on, create an ice-cold water stand, and build from there.

Never give up on dreaming, hoping, and creating something out of thin air. Life is hard in general but if you can only imagine and dream then that is where you begin. I became a master at pretending and that led me to dream big. I continue to dream big and today my big dreams have nothing to do with things or money. My wife always says, "If you ever make being financially-rich a goal, we will be set for life because you always complete your goals and reach your dreams." She knows that money does not motivate me. Today, my big dreams consist of scientists discovering cures for Multiple Sclerosis. Don't get me wrong, money is great and can bring some happiness.

"Trust no one for mankind has proven its capacity for evil over and over again. Trust not the church or man but trust in your own relationship with your God."

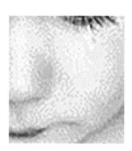

CHAPTER 9

Keeping My Head above Water

I was around the age of six, I guess, when my older brother Butch took us out to the dock on Bellevue Pond. He rowed us to the dock and he said he would take me for a ride on the boat, drop off the other kids, and he would take me back. Well, he convinced me to get on the dock so he could talk with one of his friends that were already on the dock.

Within just a few minutes, he said, "Kenny, do you want to learn to swim?"

Nervously, I said, "Yes."

He then grabbed me and threw me into the pond and he just laughed at me struggling, choking, and begging for help. At first, his friends were laughing too. But then they also began to beg Butch to help me out.

I recall with such vivid clarity Butch saying, "Don't be such a cry baby" Sounds familiar right? He then calmly said with a grin and the fiercest sky blue eyed stare if you want to get out of the water, you will have to get out yourself. It was like time stood still and all motion stopped and I could only see him watching me struggle.

Well, I did get myself on that dock and the look on the other kids' faces were horrified that Butch had the capacity to throw his six-year-old brother who never swam into a pond. So from then on, I knew that pretty much this person, who is my brother, had the capability of most anything. He just seemed to want to terrorize me every single chance he could for many years into my teens.

Reflection

Abuse comes in all forms. Emotional, physical, violence, and sexual. I endured all types of abuse at home and beyond.

This abuse was unchecked and paved the way for a decades of punishment. Take time to ask kids what their day is like. You must find time to talk because kids will rarely come out and say they are being abused, but the open discussion can lead to a discovery of bad things. Example: I, the victim of sexual abuse, may not come home and say, "Hey, everyone, the camp counselor abused me." However, if you are curious about the day, you may hear… "The counselor took me for a walk."

Open dialog builds better relationships and creates trust that must be earned when dealing with victims of abuse no matter how young or how old. The abuser works hard to instill fear so the victim remains quite.

It may sound negative not trusting anyone with your kids and you should not. I have learned that a few very powerful clues can be missed by guardians and these missed clues can be devastating and can even lead to suicide.

Once again, guilt is the driving force with almost all types of abuse. Sadly, most abuse comes from family or close family members. Of course, no one wants to talk about "family secrets" but, in my opinion, when family secrets are crimes they must be exposed. Especially when the "crime" is a violation of human rights and our moral code of conduct and values.

"Be extremely cautious of the champion of any cause. Think of it like this, a wild bear can be warm and fuzzy to look at and you may even be able to get close, and then all of a sudden you are attacked."

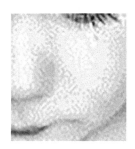

CHAPTER 10

While My Guitar Gently Weeps

 At age twelve, I was no doubt lost and unsupervised. My older sister and her boyfriend at the time, gave me a guitar to borrow so I could learn how to play. There was an older kid in the neighborhood and I was bragging about that guitar. He lured me to his house under the guise that he would teach me how to play the guitar. He helped me for a few weeks.

Then he said, "Why not leave the guitar here so you don't have to carry it home after the lesson?"

That seemed okay to me.

Then he asked if I wanted to rip-off a boat, some beer, row out to the cove island, and smoke some dope, and I said, "Sure."

I thought, *"How cool is this? I have a friend, finally."*

We did steal the boat and rowed to a small island and that is where he molested me. He gave me some pills, we smoked some pot, drank, and no need to go into detail because you get the picture. We woke up and simply rowed back to land, I went home and never told another soul in this world. I was so afraid of being in trouble. This was classic grooming, violation, and intimidation. He said that if I told anyone about what happened and ripping off the boat, that he would kick my ass and then tell everyone in the neighborhood that I was queer. Once he had that fear in me, he decided to keep the guitar and he said if I said anything about it he would tell the town about the island. To this day, I have only told one person about this crime. Now I know he was a predator monster. I knew, one day I would confront this person.

Reflection

Karma can be a bitch. But I do not condone or wish ill on anyone. You see all I wanted was my sister's guitar back or an apology, but it turned out that he perhaps got what he deserved because who knows how many others he abused. Maybe they wished him bad Karma. Either way, I am at peace with this painful secret and now my big sister and her husband finally have the truth about their guitar. I have been keeping that truth from her for forty years and it feels so good to get this off my chest. Easy to see that I waited too long but we all move at our own pace. This chapter is finally closed.

The best way I can explain how it feels to hide the truth about your abuse is like wearing a t-shirt that is way too tight, you feel so uncomfortable in your own skin that you are uneasy just stepping outside. It is like walking into a room of people and the feeling can be overwhelming. You simply decide to isolate yourself. Very un-healthy and what you learn without proper therapy is that the tight t-shirt feeling only gets tighter and tighter and then begins to morph into a full body suit of tightness. "You just can't Breath."

We should never hold on to our secret, that only enables an abuser even more. This only hurts you and empowers the abuser. Abusers thrive on making sure you keep the crime a secret. Just think of all the people that would go straight to jail if all abusers, molesters were arrested right now. The jails would be full and millions of innocent men, women, and children could begin the healing process. I say, if you know this is happening go to the police, and if you don't trust the police then go to the minister or priest, and if you don't trust anyone go to the local community center and simply ask for help. Sad, really, that the people we trust the most are often the abusers.

"You can be blessed or cursed with brothers and there is no such thing as automatic brotherly love that takes a lot of work."

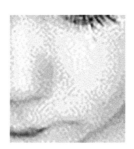

CHAPTER 11

A Wrenching Experience

Did it hurt me when my brother Butch wouldn't allow me to play football, catch, and ping-pong? You name it. He excluded me from everything. I would see my other brothers play games, hang out, laugh, and have fun. Yes, that was painful and certainly had an impact on my confidence but there are two stories that changed me in a way that I'm sure many people can understand if they come from a domestic violence environment. I was thirteen when my brother Butch came home and he accused me of stealing his cigarettes. I did not take his cigarettes but he never believed me. Later that day, he asked me for some help upstairs. I said, "Sure," and, at that point, I was hoping that it would be a good day, that there would be no violence coming my way.

As I walked up the stairs, he gave me the look that I've seen before. He grabbed me and he had a wrench that was probably three feet long. He grabbed me by the neck, hung me out the second-story window, and held onto me with that wrench. The only thing that was between that wrench and the house was my neck. I dangled two stories up. I screamed, and yelled, and begged him to stop, but it just seemed like the more I begged him to stop the harder and more violent the wrenching became. Of course, there were other siblings in the house as well as my mother but when Butch became enraged there was no one willing to get into the middle of the situation. This story is only one of many that include Butch. But this particular day out of all the abusive days had the longest negative impact on my life. You see, it wasn't exactly a very high two-story window but it was scary and that scare stayed inside of me until this day. Some laugh a little when they learn I am afraid of heights. But of course I never really tell them why, I just sort of make a few jokes on how I might hold my wife's purse while she rides the most dangerous ride at Disney. It is hard for people to imagine a black belt in martial arts that has all the confidence in the world in some areas but is absolutely terrified in other areas. But of course that is the pain that is the internal damage. The ring around my neck from the wrench certainly went away but the pain that domestic violence causes is a lifetime of internal struggle and torment.

You can imagine the fear of walking into my own home with our mother sitting right there knowing that at any given moment, for no particular reason, I was going to be abused in one way or the other. This was not new for any of us. We all saw, at one point or another, the pure violence that could come at a minute's notice. I guess the most frightening time in my life and I don't mean frightening in the moment I mean frightened to the core was when I saw Butch push my mother to the ground. This moment of anger about something so small, so ridiculous. The look in his eyes and seeing my mother on the floor is frightening and that never ever goes away. All he said was, "Sorry, Mom," and sort of helped her up. That was a glimpse of how far he would go and that terrified all of us. But for some reason Butch had me in his sights on a daily basis. Abuse of all kinds. No need to list them all, but the few I have shared gives you a picture of the domestic violence. At this point in my life, I decided to take martial arts. I joined a martial arts school and I became a stronger person, not in the sense where I was tougher or a better fighter but I simply had more confidence. That's what martial arts does, it provides each individual with a unique amount of confidence to be stronger, to be better, and not just in fighting, not just in kicking and punching. It will instill a greater burning desire to do better, to be better, and that is the platform of the man I am today.

Reflection

At that time, I only knew that it was wrong and what was happening to me should have been stopped. Now I know that abusers create an atmosphere that impacts everyone in the home. It does not have to be physical abuse. It could equally be detrimental when a spouse is being verbally abusive and or emotionally abusive. The home becomes crippled with fear and ingrains a "norm" that is distorted. In the end, human rights are at stake with all forms of abuse and those crimes and behaviors must be brought to light.

*"Big brothers are put on earth
to protect younger brothers."*

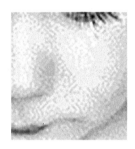

Hey, Big Brother

My brother Gus was the oldest when my father died and he was thrown into the patriarch role in our family. He helped me in many ways and I am the man I am today because of his love and care. Gus and his wife, Brenda, took me in when I was in junior high school. I was, at the time, living in Florida with my big sister and I got caught stealing a bike. I can't recall why I was in Florida away from my mother. So instead of placing me in reform school, I was sent to live with my big brother Gus, his wife, and their son.

What I thought was going to be the coolest time turned out to be a hard time. He made reform school look like club med. My big brother picked me up at the airport and I was all smiles, so to say he was pissed was an understatement. It was like he had to tear me down in every way and then build me back up. He taught me how to take care of myself, he taught me how to work, he taught me how to groom myself, and when it came time for me to go to my first dance, he dressed me in all of his clothes and, man-o-man, I looked like the coolest dude at the dance. It was a turning point in my life. I built up enough confidence to join the wrestling team and proud to say I was undefeated. I became a better person because of his love and care. He really repaired my trust in family and he never hurt me in any way.

He may have been firm but he never put his hands on me. He took me in when there was no other place to go at that time. His wife, my sister in-law, provided me with the most stable home life that I had experienced, ever. Their son was my nephew but he is more like a brother and many years later, I was so proud that my wife and I could invite him to stay with us. Talk about breaking the cycle of abuse. On the other hand, my oldest brother Gus died alone when his son found him. Sad that particular pattern was continued.

We are unsure exactly how my brother died but one thing for sure was that it was a tragic ending to a very hard life. I miss him and wish I could have been there for him in his final hours. No one deserves to die alone.

I hope you are looking down from heaven and are proud. You stood there boldly as a young man when our father died.

You deserve to rest in peace, big brother.

Reflection

Avoid the all or nothing approach with almost everything in life. This value is most important with family.

Just because one person in your family is hurtful, try not to isolate yourself from the entire family, just to avoid painful memories or to avoid that one person that hurt you. I did that. I did that in a very big way and that I regret. I thought by moving away from the history I could move away from the pain. That was and is a bad idea. Embrace those that embrace you and never let someone influence where you go.

The Lost Chapter

This is a sad part of my life. Because from age thirteen to sixteen, I just can't place myself anywhere. It's like a vortex of time in my life. Not sure what happened after living with Gus, I can't recall where I was living or what life was like from the age thirteen to sixteen. I do know that I was once again out of luck and had nowhere to stay. I do remember that for some unimaginable reason I was living with Butch, yes, sounds crazy, and it certainly proved crazier than I have ever seen.

"Family equals people you trust. Relatives equal people in your life through marriages and relationships that are not always in line with your values. The skill is to identify the difference and make a stand."

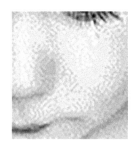

CHAPTER 13

An Ax to Grind

I was out of a job and had nowhere to go but I did get an unemployment check and he was happy to take that for letting me sleep in a room at his home. Part of my job while living with Butch was to clean and one day I was cleaning, "earning my keep" as he put it. I heard a noise in the kitchen. I walked out and what I saw with my own two eyes changed me forever. Butch was chasing his wife with an axe and he, literally, swung the axe and she moved in the nick of time. The axe was swung so hard that it actually got stuck in the floor. Sounds familiar right? How tragic the similarities with Butch and our father's violence of choice. Of course, the axe stuck in the floor made him more infuriated, and he continued to chase her and beat her. I didn't have much but what I did have I packed and left, and never said anything to anyone. Never told my mother, never told my brothers and sisters, never even spoke with him about it, I just left. Thirty-five years later, I learned that Butch was also abused by our father. No surprise. The intensity and scope I will not talk about but you can imagine. You know what they say "Like father, like son." I made peace with Butch before he died.

God have mercy on his soul.

Reflection

Regardless of who is hurting you, whether the violation is psychological abuse, physical abuse, sexual abuse, or emotional abuse, no one has the right to hurt you without being investigated by the law. Statistics show most abuses begin at home. So there is a built-in barrier to getting help. If you are young, scared, and can't trust anyone in your house to stand up for you, then you must leave no matter how young you are. I can assure you that if you walk to anyone's home begging for help because you're being abused, the "normal" family will call the police immediately. The pattern of an abuser is fear and as long as everyone around them is fearful, then the victim or victims will remain in a pattern of fear. Age has a lot to do with the ability or inability to speak out and often drives or does not drive you to get help. However, you must be strong and get help.

"Hard work pays off and it shows."

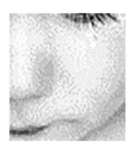

CHAPTER 14

Hard Work Pays Off

School of Hard knocks

As one of the youngest of ten children, I knew I would be on my own in many ways very early in life for many things, food, clothes, rides to lessons, fees for activities, etc. The young boy you see in this picture is me. What you can't see is the pain inside from years of torment caused by being a victim of domestic violence, physical abuse, emotional distress, sexual abuse, rape, molestation, and what amounted to abandonment.

The Complex Duplex

I knew by age thirteen that my mother would be losing more social security support as each child turned eighteen. By the time me and my siblings, Doris, David, Robert, and Barbara, were ages sixteen to seventeen, it was time to get out on our own. My mother encouraged each one of us to travel outside the small military town of North Kingstown, RI. The best job you could hope for was at Electric Boat. Shipyard work, great money, and very hard work. We all went our separate ways and we all found a place to land. I decided to quit high school and get a job because I knew independence was just around the corner. Of course, I had many jobs to include dishwasher, gas station, landscaping, and manufacturing plants. All good jobs, hard jobs, but not what I wanted for myself. I saved money and purchased my first car, a 1966 AMC Rambler Convertible. If you are unsure what AMC means, it is American Motor Company or amply nicknamed (Almost a Car).

I paid $500 for this dazzling beauty and quickly realized a little thing called "State Inspection." The front end needed a lot of work and the cost would exceed $1,200. Needless to say, I did not have the money to fix the car. So the car sat for eight months in the driveway of my sister. One would think that with seven siblings above me that I would get some help with fixing the car. However, I did not and so this just fit with my early mindset that I was on my own and had to "work" hard for everything. I resented that no one would help me because I did see other siblings getting help from each other. It was like no one cared at all and seemed that everyone was watching me struggle. That distorted perspective sort of motivated me more to get my ass in gear to get what I wanted. I can say now that my perception was in some cases right on the mark and in other cases incorrect. All of my siblings had their own challenges and outside of a few siblings, no one was in a financial position to help. I ultimately saved the money to fix the car and it was the sweetest ride you could imagine. I still enjoy the thought of that accomplishment and saved that picture.

Reflection

If you can stand it, don't help those around you when you know the person in need can help themselves. Although hard to comprehend, sometimes it is important. Many years later, I was talking with my nephew Aubrey and told him I was not going to give my sons anything without some work. He challenged me and asked, "Do you think that is necessary? Why make your kids struggle like we did?" I took that challenge and realized that I must be somewhere in the middle.

I definitely make our sons work for everything; it is just more guided lessons than I had. Quick example: In 2009, my wife and I are parents to two great kids, EJ and TY. We had a fence that needed painting every spring. So I gave both boys equal work, equal equipment, equal supplies, and equal pay. We made the agreement that I would pay each son $1 per fencepost. TY went to the left and EJ went to the right. EJ came back and asked for more paint. I said sure and refilled his paint bucket. After a while, both boys were done and payment was due. I gave TY his $8 for eight painted posts and gave EJ $6 for eight painted posts. EJ looked at me with absolute confusion. He asked me why he was paid less. I explained that TY completed the task with the materials I gave him and there is a cost to everything and he needed to be more careful. Well, the following week we had to paint the inside of the fence and I assure you that EJ finished the job well with the allotted supplies.

Now EJ is a superb employee and is always complemented on his hard work ethics.

"Influences around you don't always have to influence you in a negative way. A little bad company can push you in the right direction."

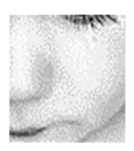

CHAPTER 15

FLORIDA or BUST!

A friend and I packed up his 1972 Monte Carlo, a rack of clothes in the back seat, a few bucks and off we went. My friend made arrangements in advance so we had a place to live. We drove to a small town in Florida. The person who ran the house met me at the door and he said, "Welcome to sunny Florida, where a lot of shady people hang out." I was clueless what that meant. It was a struggle every step of the way. It took me weeks to find a job and the guys we were staying with were all a little shady.

Reflection

Be careful who you associate with. A simple association could have landed me in jail. There were so much drugs coming in and out of the house. If it were ever raided by the police, I would have been arrested just for being in the house. Later, I learned that cocaine and marijuana were stored under the bed that I was using while staying in the house. Take very careful steps with whom you associate with. Let relationships take time. Trust no one 100 percent unless it is earned over time. After months of looking for work, I landed my first good job in Florida. I was working at TGI Fridays. Things were good. I had a new place to live, I had a truck, and things seemed to be going along well. Then my friend was moving quicker than I was with his income, and he simply moved to a new location that I couldn't afford. I found myself living with more strangers and had to get a new job because the travel to TGI Fridays was too much. The family that I was staying with also had a gas station. There I was twenty-one years old, pumping gas, and a high school drop out with a future that looked as bad as it could get. I always thought I could do better if just given a chance/window of hope and opportunity. But I never lost hope and never stopped dreaming. I was the best service station attendant you could ask for. I knew I could do better in life and I was going to stick this out and find my way.

Then one of the roommates took my car out for a ride without my knowledge and crashed it. This guy had money from a lawsuit and he paid me cash to fix the car. He gave me the cash and I thought okay, here is an opportunity. My job was a short walk away and the car was functional so I really did not have to fix the damage. I had cash and was totally optimistic that I could make something good come out of this. You see that is my nature, no matter what happens I will make it work and find something good from any situation. The next day I woke up and discovered that someone in the house stole all $1,500 of my money. That was it, I got kicked out of the house for accusing the uncle of stealing my money. I had no work or car and nowhere else to live. I was at the end of my road. Then I realized that I just signed a contract to pay $23 per month at the martial art school. I walked to the school, basically destitute, broke, and asked if I could cancel the contract.

Master Kim took over the meeting that I was having with the sales person at the school.

Master Kim said, "If you quit this, you will quit everything in your life."

I said, "How can I pay for this? I don't have a job, a place to live, I have nothing."

He said, "You have yourself and you can begin training tomorrow."

He gave me $10 and said, "Go get a haircut, come back, and you will have a place to stay, weekly pay, and a positive future."

In fact, this was a defining moment in my life. I began training as it was called. Ten-hour shifts, six days a week.

I received a stipend and lived with four to seven other trainees in a house not too far from the academy. A sort of fraternity if you will, with a single and primary goal to graduate with second degree black belt and go out in the world and teach Tae Kwon Do. Our days were filled with training, learning martial arts, and becoming adept in all aspects of operating a school. I was in the best shape of my life both physically and mentally, which was a good thing because what was just around the corner in my life would challenge everything.

Master Kim would say all the time, "Instructor Butler, physically you are the most talented martial artist I have ever seen. However, you must also master your emotions."

"Circumstances can open doors but you must walk through."

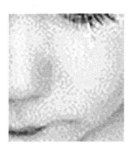

CHAPTER 16

Work, Train, Eat, Sleep

I rose to the rank of senior instructor. I taught youth classes and evening family-style classes. It was an awesome time in my life. I had a focus and a purpose.

Master Kim awarded me a scholarship. Really, a scholarship, what was I going to do with scholarship money? I did not even have a high school diploma.

1985 A.T.F. SCHOLARSHIP RESULTS ARE IN!

Another Trainee Instructor, Mr. Ken Butler also received an A.T.F. Scholarship Award earlier and has since proudly completed his secondary education earning his G.E.D. through the support and motivation of the American TaeKwon-Do Federation.

I received a scholar's award of $600. I hired a fellow classmate to prepare me for the GED test.

I worked, or as Master Kim called it "training," each day until 10:00 PM at the martial arts school. Once done there, I walked home from work with Chris Wagner, who was a student and a county jail GED instructor.

We worked every night for three months. I basically had to begin my education at an eighth grade level. It was exciting to me, and of course, the best day of my life was when my diploma arrived in the mail. I recall sharply that I was home alone when the mail came. I remember that my tutor said if the envelope is regular size that it will be bad news, but if the envelope is flat and big it will be great news. I did it! I am the proud recipient of a high school diploma. Most individuals would not hang a high school diploma up. I have won many awards, citations, certificates, and a degree, but my high school diploma is by far my greatest achievement, the one that I am most proud of. It is certainly hung with pride in my studio.

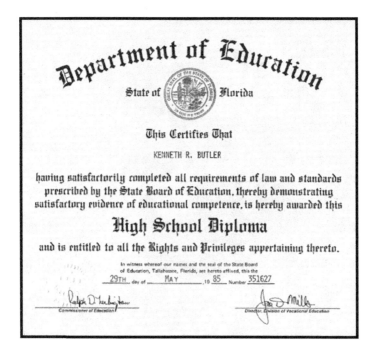

I still had one year left in my training in order to open a school but for the first time in my life, I had very strong goals that were stronger than anything else.

The impact on personal integrity and newfound confidence was so obvious. Just two and a half years earlier, I was pumping gas with no hope. But now, I had five major goals to achieve:

- Earn my high school diploma,
- Earn my second degree black belt,
- Graduate from the martial arts academy,
- Save $5,000
- Open my own school.

Before testing for second degree black belt, I went for a physical and they noticed a lump on my right testicle. They said they must do a biopsy and that I needed to come back in about four hours for the results. However, the physician said, "If I were a betting man, I will say you have cancer. We just have to determine if the tumor is malignant."

Those were the longest four hours of my life. I walked to a local lake called Lake Eola and sat there the entire time.

After all, I was in Florida by myself and I would never call my mother and say, "I might have cancer. I will call you back in a few hours." That time on that bench was important. It defined me to this day. I made a commitment that I would not take any day for granted if I lived.

I went back to the physician's office and it was there at 4:00 PM on August 29. I was wearing a tan Tae Kwon Do shirt, black sweat pants, and white sneakers when I heard those three words… "You have cancer."

What you see below is me entering my school just moments after my diagnosis.

I had to tell Master Kim and my fellow instructors that I was going to the hospital that night to get prepped for urgent surgery the very next day. This picture was taken by a student who was writing a newsletter article about my life story leading up to my graduation. Now her story was about to take on a whole different tone.

I was gearing up for the testing that I had been preparing for the last three years. I was going to graduate and open a school. In fact, I felt so strongly about graduating that I delayed the second surgery because nothing was going to get in my way of graduation.

I remember clearly the physician said, "Mr. Butler, I want to bring you up on current affairs… You have stage three cancer and we need to operate now."

I said, "No, Sir. I must graduate."

I felt the graduation was critical and I would not be denied that no matter what. The inner turmoil was intense. On one hand, I had a goal to achieve and on the other hand, I had to get ready to save my life in a battle with cancer. But I thought, *"What a shame it would be to get through all that I had endured and not achieve my goal."*

Diagnosed on August 29, 1986, and operated on the very next day to remove a malignant tumor.

The biggest day of my life and I was completely alone. This seemed to fit with who I had become. Alone and okay with it.

I recall sitting on the second floor of Humana Hospital in Orlando, Florida. I was working hard to be strong after the emergency surgery. I was drinking a cup of coffee and I took one bite of toast, and for the first time, I began to cry. The sun was out and shining on my face but I was dark and sad. Of course that only lasted five minutes because my nephew Joe came to visit. I can't imagine getting through that day without Joe by my side. He was twenty-one and I was only twenty-four but we had each other and that is what family does. As mother would always say, "We are there for each other when the chips are down."

Although the first surgery was simple, it had a complex impact on my manhood. Perhaps, similar to the way a female feels when she has breast cancer and undergoes a mastectomy. You lose a sense of your value as it relates to inherent gender pride and, for me, a struggle with masculinity.

I had no book that spoke about the physiological impact that a male experiences regarding cancer and, even deeper, how a young man diagnosed with testicular cancer copes. So I decided to write what I experienced.

For sure, having a testicle surgically removed is shocking to me. Now of course I know my value had nothing to do with my right testicle or any other body part. However, at that time in my life, it was devastating. Emotionally challenged is an understatement.

In my moments of being alone, I cried a lot. Other times I would cry during practicing Tae Kwon Do. Good thing for me I worked out all the time and I would sweat so much one could not even notice the tears. The harder I worked out, the harder I cried. I was feeling very sad about the loss of my manhood. My concern shifted very quickly to getting ready for the second more comprehensive surgery. I felt stripped, exposed, and felt less of a man. I took the time to reflect and simply found myself writing about my thoughts. The closer I got to the second surgery, the more reflective I became.

In retrospect, I really did not have adequate time between the diagnosis, the first surgery, and the second surgery. Sort of had no time to fully absorb what was happening to me.

As in the past, I had become a master at jamming emotions down and standing up to fight what was in front of me. Cancer was to me just another form of abuse. This time, the disease was the predator and I was the prey.

Of course, the formidable cancer opponent had no idea who they were dealing with. I was prepared to fight and that is exactly what I did. The fight or flight is not new but in my case, it was human nature. This was going to be the hardest fight of my life. I managed the entire circumstance with that mental focus in my mind. This was a fight and, in my mind, I broke down this fight into five rounds.

Ken Vs Cancer
Round 1
Orchiectomy

BUTLER AND HUNTER, M.D., P.A.
UROLOGY
1214 KUHL AVENUE
ORLANDO, FLORIDA 32806
(305) 843-2770

STEPHEN A. BUTLER, M.D.   PATRICK T. HUNTER, II, M.D.

September 18, 1986

RE: Butler, Kenneth

To Whom it may concern:

Mr. Kenneth Butler is a patient of mine that I have been treating since August 29, 1986. He was admitted to Humana Hospital Lucerne on the following day and underwent surgery for embryonal cell carcinoma of the right testicle. He is unable to return to work at this time, and he will probably be out for 2-3 months.

If I can be of any further help, please don't hesitate to call.

Sincerely,

Stephen A. Butler, M.D.

SAB:gr

Ken Vs Cancer
Round 2
I will not be denied.

Two weeks after the first surgery, I tested for my second degree black belt and all of the credentials to open my own school. I was not going to be denied the opportunity to test and graduate.

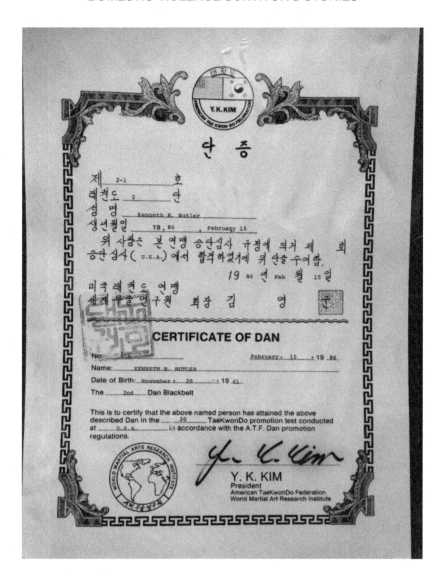

I had to have what is called a Radical Node Dissection.. This procedure is basically making an incision from your groin up to your chest, they remove all of your internal organs, and then they remove positive lymph nodes.

Ken Vs Cancer
Round 3
Radical Node Dissection

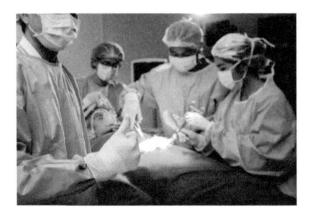

My mother, my brother Gus, and my nephew Joe were at my bed side when I woke up from this surgery. I opened my eyes after being in surgery for five hours and recovery for three hours. When I went into the surgery, they said they were not sure of the extent of the cancer. In fact, they said this was more of a cautionary measure. They in fact removed six positive lymph nodes. Four weeks after the second surgery, the chemotherapy began.

Ken Vs Cancer

Round 4

Aggressive Chemotherapy

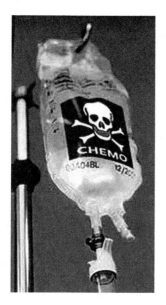

Not sure what cisplatin is or what it does to your body? Well, neither did I. Here is the profile of Cisplatin. It is an anti-cancer ("antineoplastic" or "cytotoxic") chemotherapy drug.

What Cisplatin is used for: Used to treat testicular, ovarian, bladder, head and neck, esophageal, small and non-small cell lung, breast, cervical, stomach, and prostate cancers. Also used to treat Hodgkin's and non-Hodgkin's lymphomas, neuroblastoma, sarcomas, multiple myeloma, melanoma, and mesothelioma.

Cisplatin side effects: Nausea and vomiting. Kidney toxicity. Blood test abnormalities: Low white blood cells, Low red blood cells. Peripheral neuropathy. Although less common, a serious side effect of decreased sensation and paresthesia (numbness and tingling of the extremities) may be noted. Sensory loss, numbness and tingling, and difficulty in walking may last for at least as long as therapy is continued. These side effects may become progressively more severe with continued treatment, and your doctor may decide to decrease your dose. Neurologic effects may be irreversible.

High frequency hearing loss. Ringing in the ears. Loss of appetite, taste changes, metallic taste, hair loss, your fertility, meaning your ability to conceive or father a child, may be affected by Cisplatin. Please discuss this issue with your health care provider. Nausea and Vomiting. No urine output in a twelve-hour period. Extreme fatigue, swelling, redness, and pain in one leg or arm and not the other, and yellowing of the skin or eyes.

Days before the diagnosis
July 1986

January 1987
Last day of treatment

January 1987
Two weeks after last chemotherapy treatment
Time to Feel

February 1987
One month after last treatment
Time to Heal

Ken vs. Cancer

Round 5

Taking my life back

March 1987

One month after last treatment

Time to Deal

CHAPTER 17

My Twelve Poems Inspired from Above

In the twelve months of being diagnosed, going through two surgeries, getting radical chemotherapy treatments, recovering both physically and emotionally, I was inspired in a very spiritual way unlike any other time before or after the illness. I wrote what I believed to be God-sent inspirations. This may sound corny but when I wrote each and every time it was like God was talking to me and I was writing based on his grace, power, and wisdom.

I am Ready, Lord

Oh my God hear my cry, please take my soul if
I should die. If it is your will that my body perish or remain, my trust in thee is the same.

The First Day of Chemotherapy

The first treatment will start only with the Lord. Without Him, we could not afford to be as strong. He will make it quick and short instead of painful and long. Cancer is on the inside but so is our Lord. We must always remember he is with us on each accord. Remember that he loves us; remember we need him. He will lead us to the father in the sky. Remember never ask him why. Only to the Lord, we could never lie.

The Second Day of Chemotherapy

Lord, I believe you see the physical and mental pain that is ahead for me. Please give me the wisdom that my sickness is like the transient rain. Please give me humbleness not to be vain. Let my faith grow to the highest high. Help me seek the kingdom in the sky. Teach me never to ask why. Open your heart to sing your song, always, always be strong.

Alone

I am alone it seems like all the time not only my body but in my mind. Why must I always look for something to do or someone to talk to? This I have always wondered, how about you?

The Pain

The pain is like the rain, only God controls it, Some men fear it, some men try to escape it, some men take it, and aimless men walk in it, Foolish men play in it but this man deals with it.

Friends in the Cancer Jail

Yes, my friends, be strong. Like your stay, our life is not very long. So if you're down, remove the frown, and dream of the day when you exchange our cross for our crown. This, you carry your whole lifelong. Sometimes our crosses are filled with sorrow and sometimes our crosses are filled with songs. So with all your heart thank God for today and pray your heart will not be chilled. This may mean a little or this may mean a lot, but the cross my friend is the best thing we've got. So carry it proud whether you're stuck in the cancer jail or getting out. Jesus did for us, is not that what our life is all about? So never leave the word, sing, scream, and shout, let all men know what your life is about.

The Finish

Life is like a vapor and death is just one part of human nature. When no one is sure, how is the same and why is easy, so we can go on to a better place. This is called the human race. After you start and where you finish is all predetermined, and what direction you run, toward the darkness or toward the sun.

The Next Procedure

People are such as a blade of grass if they grow to a boastful size they will be cut down in a flash.

However, the roots remain and the next procedure is the same. So try to grow on the inside, not out and not up but stay low on the out and high on the in so the next procedure will never begin.

Imagine

Just what would we do if we only had thirty minutes to live. What you would do first is normally what we would do last in our everyday life. So do the things that you would normally save for last and do them today. Imagine every day is your last day but is also your very best day.

What If

Things of the earth are heavy and hard. Just what would we do if it sank beneath the tar? Yes, all things like the tree and the flower, yes, my friend even the hour. Yes, we would all cry, surely we would all cry to the heavens and the sky. Oh my God, please take me I'm sure men would say but the men who are heard will be the men who pray.

The Last Day of Chemotherapy

My life is a gift and that gift is encouraged through the human spirit. That is the thing that will carry me all the days God has given me. I have only one thing to share with the world and that one thing is my life. Finally, I'm not alone and if and when I am alone I will embrace it with all my heart because it is that place where I learned so much about living. Imagine that in learning about dying I have learned more about living.

Remorse Not

The woods are dark yet they inspire hope

The woods are bright yet they can steal the light

The woods are full yet they are not crowded

The woods are cold yet they are full of warmth

The woods are lonely yet they are full of good company. Remorse not we that made it out of the woods

The reason we made it out is not for us to question. However, that we have made it out of the woods, we must help those who are still in the woods

We must help those who are just entering the woods

We must help those who have to go back to the woods

Most of all, we must remember our friends that never had the chance to walk in the woods.

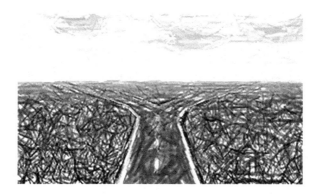

I know now that I would have to retrain myself and go back to school.

You see, while I was out of work going through surgeries and chemotherapy, I had two other great things happen in my life.

I met my future wife, as she was my nurse.

I decided to go to college and pursue my love of art.

One would think that after earning my GED that I would head straight for college. Well I did not as my other major goal was to open a school and I was working hard to make that dream come true. Once the trauma of being diagnosed with cancer settled in and I decided to fight and survive, I had some serious time for reflection.

Beth and I set up our life in Orlando. Then the college I chose was in Ft. Lauderdale. I worked full time in a warehouse and went to school full time. Beth was also working full time at a local hospital. We learned very early that because we were so far from family, we relied on each other for everything. We worked hard to build a life together.

CHAPTER 18

Our Love Story

 I attempted to go through chemotherapy by myself while I was living in Central Florida. Well, I failed at that. I was just not physically able to take care of myself and get back and forth to chemotherapy so I decided to head back home to Rhode Island. I stayed with my mother and my brother David in a very tiny apartment. It reminded me of the old days when everyday mom had at least ten to fifteen people playing cards or just dropping in to say "Hi" and have "a coffee."

My second treatment was administered at Roger Williams Hospital. At the time, it was a teaching hospital and I had a crew of ten physicians and residents picking, poking, pulling, and helping me get through the grueling six-day twenty-four by seven IV drip. Cysplatnum was the main drug at the time for my type of cancer. In fact, I saved the last sticker on the bag of this toxic medicine or poison as I now call it. More about the impact that drug had on my life in later chapters.

One day, I had such a terrible reaction to the treatment that I had to go back to hospital. The cancer ward was full so they said I would have to go on the medical surgical floor until a bed opened up on the cancer ward. I said, "Whatever you need to do," just to get some relief.

You see the chemotherapy was so aggressive that it made me sick for days. There was constant vomiting and of course after a while there was nothing more to vomit so I began to cough and gag so much that my eyes had so many broken capillaries from the constant pressure of throwing up. My eyes were red. I just wanted to get some relief. Once admitted to my room, in she walked. I knew in a matter of minutes that she would be my wife. She just did not know it yet. I asked Beth to dinner and we dated the entire time I was going through treatment.

Below is the sticker from the last bag of the intravenous medicine.

Beth was there to take me home at one in the morning because I was leaving the hospital once I was unhooked from that last bag. Beth knew I would do it on my own and she decided to come back after working a twelve-hour shift and took me out of that hospital.

So I was done with the entire process of being diagnosed, two surgeries, and six months of chemotherapy. Time to get back to Florida and get my life back. By this time, Beth and I made plans that she would come with me. She had some trouble convincing her parents that it was a good thing for her to fall in love with a guy that was sick and lived in another state. I went back to Florida. Beth and I began our long distance relationship for the next six months. Of course I had to face the fact that it was time to go back to work.

The letter that my physician had to write that explained why my life had to change.

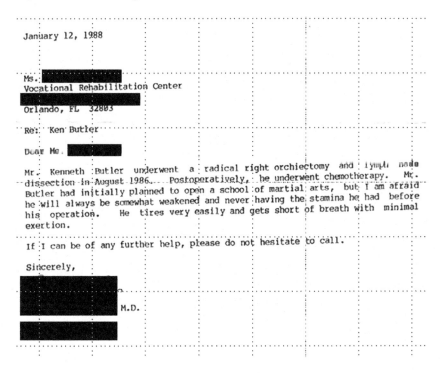

January 12, 1988

Ms. ▮▮▮▮▮▮▮▮▮▮
Vocational Rehabilitation Center

Orlando, FL 32803

Re: Ken Butler

Dear Mr. ▮▮▮▮▮▮

Mr. Kenneth Butler underwent a radical right orchiectomy and lymph node dissection in August 1986. Postoperatively, he underwent chemotherapy. Mr. Butler had initially planned to open a school of martial arts, but I am afraid he will always be somewhat weakened and never having the stamina he had before his operation. He tires very easily and gets short of breath with minimal exertion.

If I can be of any further help, please do not hesitate to call.

Sincerely,

▮▮▮▮▮▮▮▮▮▮ M.D.
▮▮▮▮▮▮▮▮▮▮

Beth traveled back and forth from RI to Florida multiple times. Everyone said she was crazy to get involved with me while in the hospital and certainly had no support dating me while she was in RI and I was back in Florida.

We dated and then started our life together in Central Florida. We lived together for about a year and then we selected a date that we were to be married.

I returned to work and got a full time job in a warehouse. Although the physician wrote I would never be the same, I was saving for my school. But that goal became less likely and I wanted to go to college with the guidance from my future father-in-law, who was at the time a principal of a high school in New England. He shuffled me in with the other high school kids taking an aptitude test for the military. Best advice I ever got. I decided on an art school in South Florida where I earned a degree in Advertising Design.

Thank you Ted for letting me marry your daughter and secondly for helping me with my career choice. My father-in-law is one of two people in my life that I know has dedicated their life to one profession and the other person is my wife. This was a glimpse of the dedication that my wife has and she has shown that in every aspect of her life.

I decided on a college in South Florida so Beth and I packed up what little we had and relocated to Ft. Lauderdale, FL. I was working and going to college earning a degree in Advertising Design.

Beth was working at a large hospital. We were saving and working for our wedding day that was planned for October 7, 1988, and then, bridge over troubled waters was on the horizon.

College was hard for me. I did very well with the art of course, but the academics pushed me to work hard. I worked hard enough to be on the Dean's list and joined the Perfection Club. The Perfection Club is where you earn a perfect 4.0 and, for me, a high school dropout, this was and is a big deal. Beth supported me every step of the way. In fact, Beth even finished my final Fine Arts term paper. In the next chapter you will learn why Beth had to finish my final paper on history of art.

In the next chapter, I write about a troubled young man that grew into a grown man with addictions that he could not control.

CHAPTER 19

Bridge over Troubled Waters

Beth had to complete my final term paper because I was dealing with the death of a sibling.

How does one cope with a sibling's suicide? The story of David.

Dave was like many other kids in the late 70s and early 80s. He was a young man that was always hanging around the "Older Crowd." Parties, girlfriends, travel, you name it. Dave had full freedom. One afternoon, I am sure between the hours of 3 pm to 6 pm, Dave begins his exploration with drugs. He was to me the coolest guy in town. Hitchhiking around town, getting into bars, dating older girls and of course heavily influenced by our older brother Butch and other "friends."

He was like the rest of us in the family, tormented by the loss of our father. By the time he was eighteen, he had consumed and experimented with the harshest of drugs. Then one night, he drove home under the influence of God knows what. He flipped his car over and was thrown out of the car.

It was right in front of his apartment and the police could not find him. He was thrown so far that he was not found with ease. He had no broken bones, no large lacerations, and no major blood loss. He did however have a small tear on his ear, and what would be obvious later was that Dave suffered a serious brain injury in the crash.

Dave was in a coma for weeks and the neurologist said it is not likely he will recover and may never wake up. His brain was bruised very badly.

So we prayed…

and prayed some more.

Miraculously David woke up from his coma. Then the physicians said Dave would not walk again due to the brain injury.

So we prayed…

and prayed some more.

Then Dave began to walk and then the neurologist said it is not likely he would regain his speech due to the brain injury.

So we prayed…

and prayed some more.

Then Dave began to talk and the neurologist said it is not likely he would return to work.

So we prayed…

and we prayed some more, and David returned to his government job.

Dave worked hard to get the rest of his life back together.

The neurologist said the part of Dave's brain that was bruised needs to heal and drugs and alcohol would only delay or block repair all together.

So we prayed…

and prayed a lot more but unfortunately for Dave what the neurologist said this time was 100 percent accurate.

Dave went back to work just fine, would walk all over town with a pronounced limp, and slipped right back to his old addictions. I do mean right back to his life, including drugs, alcohol and hanging with his "friends."

In a little over a five-year period, from 1982 through 1988 after that crash, Dave returned to all of his addictive habits. The neurologist predicted that Dave would become a paranoid schizophrenic and that is exactly what happened to Dave. He began to hear voices and was struggling in every way.

I recall one time he came into a pizza joint in town and he sat down with me and my older brother and began to yell at my father's image that Dave saw in the corner. He was using such bad language that it was scary to me. In retrospect, I should have done more that night and in general. If I only had the insight that I do now with the nature of intervention, I would have taken more action. This is not to say my other siblings did not do all they could for David. In fact, he was Bailer Acted several times at the hand of our family. Like all addicts, he was the master at getting into rehab but also the grand master at getting out. His compulsion to use drugs was just that strong. In addition, his friends, close relatives and Butch contributed to his addictions.

He was on so many very strong medications, it reminded me of how animals looked and acted when tranquilized. He no longer had the essence of himself. The voices and the noises in his head became too much for David.

The newspaper clipping below is what our family was forced to read in a local paper about our dear David.

E-4   MONDAY, SEPTEMBER 19, 1988

Man's body found at Jamestown Bridge

The body of David V. Butler, 29, of 170 Heritage Rd., North Kingstown, was discovered Saturday near the Jamestown Bridge in Narragansett Bay.

Jamestown police said the body was sighted by a fisherman about 11:15 a.m., floating about 20 feet from the Jamestown shore. It did not appear the body had been in the water for a long time.

Police said they were awaiting autopsy results to determine the time, cause and circumstances of death.

Mr. Butler, a lifelong North Kingstown resident, was a welder for Electric Boat's submarine-building yard at Quonset Point.

Born in South Kingstown, he was a son of Elizabeth (Potter) Butler of North Kingstown and the late Aubrey G. Butler Sr.

Besides his mother he leaves four brothers, Aubrey G. Butler of Wakefield, Lloyd Butler of Coventry, Kenneth Butler in Florida and Robert Butler in North Carolina; and five sisters, Rosemary Case of West Warwick, Lois Fuscaldo and Norma Johnson, both of North Kingstown, Doris Crump in North Carolina and Barbara Stinnett in Ohio.

The funeral will be held Wednesday at 11 a.m. in the Lawrence E. Fagan Funeral Home, 825 Boston Neck Rd. Burial will be in Elm Grove Cemetery.

Very sad ending for a beautiful person. No words can describe the feeling of losing a sibling, and to lose a sibling to suicide is just such a raw emotion that can't heal in my opinion. We are just not wired for such a tragedy.

We are just not wired to lose a sibling and to lose a sibling in this manner is just very hard to deal with.

I miss Dave every single day and only wish I did more to help. I have told this story many times to middle school students and youth organizations such as the YMCA and Martial Arts programs. Each time, I ask if they thought Dave was strong-willed or not. Often the reaction is mixed. I always say this…

David survived

- A near fatal car crash at sixty MPH
- Getting thrown forty feet and landed on his head
- Battled a coma
- Suffered brain damage

- Fought back from partial paralysis
- Endured months of physical rehabilitation and speech therapy
- Conquered occupational therapy
- Experienced social ridicule

Yes, I would say that Dave was strong-willed indeed. More so than any other person I have ever met in my life. But what Dave could not control was his desire for drugs and alcohol. You see that is the biggest gamble you will ever take. Some folks can smoke pot, drink a little now and then, and never have an issue. Others take one toke, take one drink, and lose the will to stop. Some folks just can't control it and that is what happened to Dave. Although he knew the risks with his continued use of drugs and alcohol, he just could not stop to save his own life.

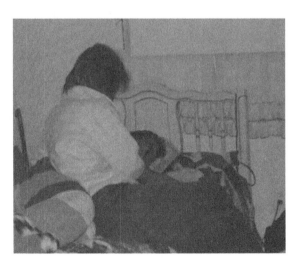

My wife Beth comforting Dave in some of his darkest hours before his death. Beth had a way with Dave that just made him laugh. Many years after David's suicide, I was crying one night in bed. I asked my wife this question as she held me close. I asked, "Why can't

I get over the loss of David? No matter what positive things were happening in my life, the first thing that was on my mind when I woke up was David." My wife gave me this advice, she said, "You are not expected nor are you supposed to get over the death of a sibling. You do have to learn new ways to cope."

From that moment on, I began to paint and carve seashells with a theme of lighthouses. I chose the theme of lighthouses because I want to believe the last thing Dave saw in this wonderful world was the lighthouse that was very close to the bridge where he committed suicide. Of course I have no way of knowing if he jumped off the south side or the north side but this is my way of paying tribute to Dave. It provides me with peace and a new way to "cope."

When asked why I don't sign my lighthouse works, my answer is, "If you know, you know." Friends that receive a shell are those I have shared the story of Dave with so they know the reason and the reason outweighs my name on it. I hope this art and the reason behind the art spreads joy. No matter what life is hitting you with and in the darkest hours of anyone's desperation or depression, they see some joy in this world.

Reflection

If you have lost a sibling or anyone else, I encourage you to seek professional counseling and find some way to express those feelings such as drawing, writing, singing, running, jogging, etc. Find something that does not hurt you or anyone else and funnel that energy that will never go away into something positive.

The coolest guy I ever knew
In loving memory of our sweet and loving brother, David.
We all miss you very much!

I learned through David's actions to always stand by family. He was loyal and I have always said this about my brother David. "If you were against him you could not win, but if you were with him you could not lose."

*"Be honest with yourself and the
window to your life will be clear."*

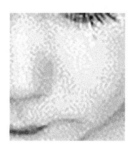

CHAPTER 20

Rise and Fall

The death of David was devastating and we all had to go back to our life. Never quite the same in our hearts and minds. Beth and I were living in Florida, we both had good jobs. For the first time in my life, I was settling down. I did not have to worry about food or shelter, I owned my home. I graduated from college, got a great job, and all was going so well. But one day, I just could not get out of my robe and go to work. I had been burying the pain and sorrow for many years and I guess when I could finally relax, my mind would not allow the suppression to continue. I did not return to work and began therapy for depression. I was thirty-three and all of a sudden my emotional state was that of a six-year-old boy. Sort of hit an emotional road block at age thirty-three.

One night after working a sixteen-hour day in a retail department store in the advertising department, I was heading to my car that was parked under the highway in Miami, Florida. I stopped and noticed a homeless man that was covered up in a newspaper. Not so significant but what I saw was three months of my hard work designing newspaper ads that was being used as a temporary blanket, and in a day or two my work would be completely disintegrated, epiphany is an understatement. That one moment made me realize I was not living the life I wanted. I made a commitment to myself that after surviving cancer I would not spend a minute of my life doing something that did not fulfill my spirit.

I could not go to sleep that night because I knew that I was not returning to that job no matter what.

I could not fall asleep and my wife woke up and found me in my robe crying, shaking, and in what I thought was a depressed state. I decided to seek therapy as the burst of sadness was too much for me to handle. The hardest part was everything was great. I had a good job, a new bride, a house, cars, and money to enjoy life.

I crashed or, a better analogy could be, I sank to the bottom.

I began my treatment with a therapist that we had in our health insurance plan. No need for me to resign the job I did not like. I was on medical leave.

The therapist was talking more about her issues than mine. After a few weeks, she asked me for my help. The therapist borrowed money from me and continued using my credit card number to rent cars with it. My wife being a health care professional was furious. She wanted to press charges but I just wanted to get away.

About this time, I called my older brother Gus because I was still in a depressed state of mind and the therapist simply caused me to go deeper in isolation. I called my oldest brother one night because I had hit the bottom with my own depression. Years of pushing down the pain that comes with domestic violence, abuse, neglect, the death of our brother Dave, and my cancer was overwhelming. I called my oldest brother because he was also like my father. That too was eating at me, the loss of a father is hard, and it all catches up to you. So here

I am calling my brother for moral support, and it turned into this lifelong confession of a dark secret he had carried his entire life.

He told me that on the day of my father's passing, he had to go and identify the body, and what he discovered was hell. He saw prescription drugs and alcohol bottles everywhere in the apartment. I was shocked, that my father took his own life, on purpose or otherwise, it was devastating.

I was shocked to learn this about my father and that news pushed me down even more. During the therapy, I did remember trauma in my past, aka posttraumatic stress disorder. I was allowing memories to return and one that was particularly troubling involved me being molested.

Knowing that I cannot call my older brothers and would not burden my younger brother with my issues, I decided to call a relative. I wanted to ask if he could help me track someone down because I learned that confronting the person who abused you is healthy.

I asked this relative to track down this dirt bag. He found the person and the person was dead. He drowned. My brother in-law said, "The world has a way of weeding out the bad people."

Reflection

Get help! But search and basically interview your therapist and in today's world you can search the credentials to ensure you are picking a therapist that is not crazy like the one I had thirty years ago. There are so many people that struggle with mental health and it is just not okay. The dysfunction continues if untreated no matter what the issues are. I continue therapy today but having the correct diagnosis is key to learning effective coping skills.

There is a huge difference between depression, anxiety, and posttraumatic stress disorder, and if misdiagnosed or untreated can cause tremendous pain and suffering. There are highly skilled professionals that can help us. I have met folks that place all their recovery needs in treatment with groups or churches or someone. I say, use all methods of recovery. No need to replace one addiction with another. So for example some folks just seek religion as a way to dig out, then once the regular support of the church, the group, the friend, or whatever, is gone you are left with yourself. The constant external support cannot be sustained over time. In my opinion, you must learn how to stand on your own while surrounding yourself with people for support. Seek professional counseling and learn how to self-motivate and cope, and stay with therapy as long as it takes. I know insurance policies these days have limits, but if you are mentally ill, you must push for those limits.

Once again, I trusted someone and twenty years later was accurately diagnosed with PTSD. So not only was this person a thief, a liar, and a cheat, she was a terrible therapist. I am not suffering from depression.

Yes, maybe I get depressed but the underlying psychosis is PTSD and for the first time in my life, it felt clear and I finally prepared to begin the real steps that come with the correct diagnosis of posttraumatic stress disorder.

It took 25 years for me to decide that I needed therapy. At age thirty-three, I was misdiagnosed and mistreated by the therapist.

It took me approximately another 25 years to get to the point where I really needed help and now that I have been properly diagnosed, I can begin to heal and I can begin to feel better inside. Because in the end no matter what's going on in our life, we all just want to feel better somehow someway and until that happens most of us won't stop or most of us find ways to feel better. People suffering from PTSD will turn to drugs, alcohol, or whatever it takes to relieve that pain, suffering, and agony. For me, I found writing and now therapy. It is hard and when you just keep piling it on year after year, anguish after anguish, it all catches up to you no matter how strong you think you are. I hit a wall.

Most people in my life describe me as the most positive person they have ever met. My wife of course sees the most complex man that I am. Well I am here to tell you it is a persona that I have mastered until now. One can argue that it is a state of denial or being fake. I say, "It is just me trying to be positive and if acting positive keeps me from being sad, I will do whatever it takes." Some days are good and some days not so much, but like my wife always says, "You have to learn new ways to cope." With the right therapist you can begin the healing process and develop new coping skills.

"Wherever you go, there you are."

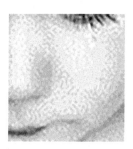

CHAPTER 21

Left a Good Job in the City Heading North

I had the best job in the world in Coconut Creek, Florida, but something was missing in our life. Children. One big hurdle was that cancer treatment made me unable to have children.

After years of trying to become parents failed, Beth and I decided to go home. We thought if we are not going to be parents, let's at least be around family.

We sold our home in Florida, then moved to New Hampshire, then sold our home in New Hampshire, and relocated to Rhode Island.

Life was lots of fun, we had a corvette and a motorcycle. We enjoyed trips and was actually planning to retire early. Then we decided to adopt a son. This decision was harder than one would imagine. Cancer took my chances of becoming a parent biologically. The process was hard because I linked all my thought patterns around how adopting would not allow me to pass any of my genes on, as that is part of being a man. Beth and I struggled with getting pregnant.

We just thought it would be easy. Having foresight, my physician said I should consider freezing sperm. before the second surgery and chemo. I did that and now we began in vitro fertilization. Outside of being very expensive, it was very emotional for us. My wife had to get shots and this process impacts females in a dramatic hormonal way. Not to get into the science of it all but the process mimics being pregnant and when it did not work it was a sad time indeed.

Once we finally decided not to continue trying IVF, we quickly realized that we still wanted to be parents.

After months of recovering and thinking about adopting, we made the decision to adopt.

Now the question was would we adopt domestically or internationally? I was still struggling with not passing my genes to the next generation.

Then Beth said, "Who had the most impact on your life?"

I said, "Master Kim, my Tae Kwon Do teacher."

She said, "He does not have a gene connection to you and you love and respect him just as much as if he were related to you."

At that moment, we decided to adopt from Korea. Master Kim saved my life so we thought we could be part of a child's life and the connection with Korea was natural.

Now making the choice to adopt is only one small step. This takes a lot of money. At that time, the expenses exceeded $20,000. We saved and finally the day came when EJ Butler became part of our life.

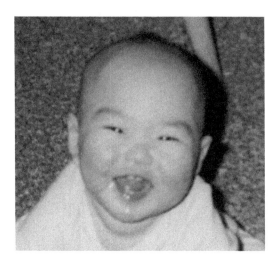

EJ arrived in 2000 and life was grand! Adoption was the best thing we ever did. If you have ever wanted something so much and then thought it would never happen that is exactly what we were thinking. Life was not so perfect just yet.

Since we wanted to be closer to family, we sold our home in New Hampshire and relocated to Rhode Island. I left RI when my brother Dave was still recovering from his car crash and you can imagine all the other reasons I left and did not want to return. But this was the only way to salvation. I was to return and face all of the demons that I tried to get away from.

I had this great job all lined up at the YMCA before we relocated. I was ready to dedicate my life to something bigger than myself. I wanted to be the best YMCA person one could find. I was teaching Tae Kwon Do, managing the fitness center, and was also the after school director. All of this while our son EJ attended preschool right at the YMCA where I was working at. It became clear to Beth that EJ should have a sibling. So we decided to adopt another child.

We adopted another child and his name is TY.

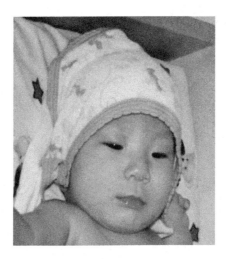

TY arrived to us when he was only four months old. He too was at the YMCA. Our life was great but as indicated earlier I would not spend time doing anything that did not fulfill my spirit. It was time for me to move on from my work at the YMCA. As you can imagine, I had the opportunity to help so many people in the community. I wanted to try corporate fitness.

This job opened up at a large corporate wellness firm based in New York. I was assigned to manage an onsite wellness center at a Fortune 100 organization. This was another ideal job for me. Helping employees get healthy while in the middle of their workday was fantastic.

I was hired in March of 2006 and I was so proud of this new job. The YMCA was great but this job was the pinnacle in my opinion. And in just three weeks from starting this new exciting job, something would happen that changed me, once again, forever.

First day of the new job

In December of 2005, my older brother Butch died of a massive heart attack. I was certain I was healthy but we did have a family history of heart disease. I decided to get checked out.

"Trust your instincts, they are almost always correct."

CHAPTER 22

Serious as a Heart Attack

My seven years of work at the YMCA came to a close. I was once again in the very best shape of my life. I got my fighting weight back at a hundred and eighty-five. I was lean and ready. Two weeks into my dream job, I woke up at midnight and could not breathe.

Okay, here is the back story. In December of 2005, my older brother dies from a massive heart attack at his home. I knew I was healthy and wanted to get everything checked. I have a history of heart disease in my family. I had every single test known to cardiologists. I had a Thallium Stress test, EKG, blood work, the works.

The doctor said, "Mr. Butler, you are in superb condition for a forty-eight-year-old man and everything is okay, you do have slightly elevated cholesterol but we can correct that with Crestor."

Okay, sounds good to me.

Fast forward only ninety days later on April 21, 2006, I woke up and could not breathe. I live in a rural setting and I knew that if I called EMS, I may not make it. I woke up my wife, we got our sons up, and Beth drove me to the hospital. Breathing became so hard I had to lean all the way back in my car seat and rumble my lungs to get air. We walked into the lobby of the hospital and that is where I actually had the heart attack, in the lobby in front of my wife and kids. Obviously I was angry that just ninety days earlier I was "Fine Mr. Butler" and then now I practically almost died on my couch at home. Fair warning that this information is exactly what was told to me and is in no way my medical opinion.

The next day I wanted answers. I found myself being prepped for "catheterization."

Once again, lucky is not the word for it. Here is how the conversation went.

"Can someone tell me how I can be fine Mr. Butler in January and practically die on my couch in April?"

"Well, Mr. Butler, it appears that your descending main artery is 99 percent blocked."

So I asked, "How can this be if I was okay ninety days ago?"

Get this, they said all of the tests we did will only show a 70 percent block or more. Because most people die within a few seconds with that much blockage.

"Okay, so why did I survive?"

He said, "Because of your vigorous exercise habits, you have many collateral arteries that create many little roads around the block."

"Okay, so what you are saying is that I may have been 70 percent blocked in December and in just ninety days became completely blocked?"

He said, "Yes, and that is why what you had is called the widow maker, most people die."

"Okay, so what you are saying is that the thing I have done most of my adult life in an attempt to be healthy practically killed me?"

"Yes."

"Okay, now how can I tell if the blockage is occurring in my body and if my body is telling me something is wrong what shall I do?"

"Be in tune to how you feel."

"Okay, so what you are saying is the remedy is that I have to be more in tune with my body?"

Really, I am very in tune with my body. After cancer, if I have a bump, lump, or anything I get it checked out. Now I am relegated to taking sixteen medications daily. Crazy right, but without these medications I will simply die way too young.

By the way, the only way to see if my heart is getting blocked is to get a catheterization, but it is considered a procedure and not a test. Insurance will not pay for it unless it is an emergency. Talk about living on eggshells.

So basically I have to practically die and actually have another heart attack before I can get a catheterization. I recovered and was out of work for twelve weeks. When I got back to work, I worked hard to change even more, to live a healthy lifestyle. About a year passed and then I was diagnosed with Type II diabetes.

CHAPTER 23

Ticking Time Bomb

So here I am a fitness professional and, due to what I think is hereditary heart decease, now diagnosed with Type II diabetes. Embarrassed is an understatement.

So being the good patient, I was attending diabetic training classes at the hospital where I had the first heart attack. On my way out of the training, I feel this pinching in my chest. So not wanting to be a whiner, I called my wife and said I was having chest discomfort. I explained to her that I was having these pinching feelings in my chest.

She said and I quote, "Don't be an idiot, you're in a hospital, just ask for help."

I said, "Well you know, I don't want to ask for help. With my history of having heart disease, everyone will get excited and then the next thing you know I'm in the hospital for heartburn."

So Beth said, "Why not just go to the doctor's? It's right around the corner."

I got in the car and drove to my doctor's office. I walked in and within sixty seconds, I was in the exam room. I had a complete heart-related episode. I passed out and needed nitroglycerin. They called 911 and it brought me back to the hospital. Yup, that afternoon I was in surgery for another 99 percent block, this time I had two stents put in.

Lucky again. The surgeon said, "I'm not sure why you are alive and certainly not sure how you could be walking around with that much blockage."

I was out of work for another six to eight weeks. The doctor said many people do not go back to work after this type of medical condition. Well, not working for me would be like punishment. So I pressed on and returned to work. In fact, that year I won awards for leadership and proficiency in team building.

Seemed like death had escaped me once again. Me, Beth, EJ, and TY enjoyed more time as a family. We went camping and did that for many years. Life was great. We went camping almost every weekend for four years.

This was the best time of our life as a family.

We watched our boys grow up and camping became the thing we worked hard for.

CHAPTER 24

Riding Along in My Automobile

I was all set to not ride my motorcycle on Memorial Day weekend in the summer of 2012 and few of my buddies wanted me to go get my bike. It was 8:30 am and a remarkable sunny day. I was heading east and the other driver was heading west. Everyone was doing their part and all of sudden, WAM! He hit me! He came so far into my lane that the impact occurred on my right side shoulder line. The impact spun my car around and I was heading east alright, but I was rolling backward at fifty-five MPH.

In just five seconds…

1. The realization I was going to get hit
2. The crash occurred
3. The airbags went off
4. The car rolled backwards fifty feet into oncoming traffic

The car stopped and I was trapped inside and I saw smoke coming out of the engine compartment. I was in a panic, I thought for sure I was going to burn up in my car. Of course, my first instinct was to call my wife and that is what I did.

While I was on the phone with Beth, panicking, the fire captain tapped on my window and asked if I was alright.

I said, "Yes, I just can't get out."

He looked at me with those eyes of a grandfather with a hint of "Are you serious expression" and said. "Relax and put your car in park."

Of course the doors will not open if your car is in drive but then again I was never in a crash so this was all new to me. I got out of the car and was ready to waive medical.

My wife drove up and she said, "Oh, you will get in that ambulance to get checked out."

Well, long story short, classic whiplash and then major back surgery 4 years later. On December 22, 2016 I had to have what is called anterior and posterior lumbar fusion that included 4 months of recovery. However, the haunting and lingering side effect of the car crash is the fear when I drive that the next car may be that car that hits me. All the horrors that I have faced can't compare to the constant fear that someone else will be texting about who knows what and risk their life and my life due to a distraction. The real danger is when you take your eyes off the road for anything and the others around are out of control. Please turn your phones off while driving. How sad would it be if you killed someone while texting mundane messages that can wait!

Reflection

Go with your gut, your instincts, vision, or whatever you may call it, that little voice in your head. I should have listened to that voice and never changed plans to go bike riding that day.

Many weeks later, my son and I were passing the spot of the crash. He asked me, "Dad, why did you have to get hit?"

Always being positive for my sons, I said, "Maybe the car behind me had a small child in the car and I got hit to save the child. Maybe it was an older person in the car behind me." I said, "We have to trust that God has the reason."

He looked at me and said, "So you took the hit, right, dad?"

I said, "Yes, I took the hit."

CHAPTER 25

The Summer of 2014

My dear wife was diagnosed with MS in June 2014. She had many small signals that we missed, such as the feeling of restless leg syndrome, slight balance issues, and left hand grip weakness. All silent symptoms of MS. One day, she had a girls' day at our home and one of her friends she had not seen in some time saw Beth walk and instantly asked, "Are you limping?" Thank you, Toni!

Beth said, "I have a little limp but I did hurt my foot."

The friend said, "Have you gotten checked out for MS?"

After weeks of tests and examinations, it was in fact MS. Just like that, our world changed forever.

I don't like to admit this but I became very depressed and here is how it happened. First, I got very sad for my wife because she is the type of lady that will keep her pain to herself and I realized she would "suffer in silence."

Secondly, sad for our children because we always tell them the truth and this was going to be no different. Beth's aunt had MS and was in a wheelchair for many years before she passed away. Beth's uncle took care of his wife and that thought came into my mind many years earlier. I wondered what kind of husband I would be if Beth became ill. *Could I be strong enough?* It seems selfish that Beth's diagnosis triggered a very deep depression in me.

So, as I have in the past, I sought therapy and it turns out that spouses are impacted in a traumatic way and my depression was simply part of the process when your life partner has been diagnosed with a serious illness. To learn your life partner has a potentially disabling disease simply does not have reference points.

One weekend, we were having a blast at a Jimmy Buffet concert and the next thing you know you are faced with the realization that your wife has a potentially disabling condition.

Thinking back, she had been saying her leg was jumpy and at times she would be off balance. Scary times!

Me and PTSD

This time, the treatment focused on how to cope with a spouse that is diagnosed with a serious illness. Beth always took care of me. Cancer, heart attacks, depression, diabetes, auto accident, and day-to-day support. Now I felt helpless in every single aspect of support-ing her in her time of need. That of course made me more depressed that I somehow focused on me and then the spiral began. I felt bad for my wife, then I felt bad that I was getting depressed, and the cycle went round and round until I sought professional help again. As you recall, I had at one point sought counseling. The therapist took advantage of me and my good nature, borrowed money, and used my credit card for personal purposes. So there really were many things that had just gotten pushed down even further.

With so much buried beneath the surface, I finally received the correct diagnosis. I am not depressed, I have finally been properly diagnosed and treated with posttraumatic stress disorder. I chose to illustrate the records on my medical diagnosis because of two reasons.

First, I have nothing to hide. In fact, this is the issue in our society. We simply hide these things as if it were our fault. No more shame for me and no more hiding. I view these documents as proof of the battles that I am most proud of.

Second, in recent history, there have been some very dishonest and despicable people in the world that have written about things that are just fiction. That dishonesty marginalizes the real fighters and survivors that are down and out, dealing with a crisis and the highly functioning individuals with mental illness.

LICSW

Office:

January 28 2016

Dear Mr. Butler,

Per your request, this letter confirms your treatment with me beginning on 8/20/14 with our last session being on 4/1/15. During our work together, the focus of treatment was on managing symptoms of anxiousness, sadness, hopelessness, and processing childhood traumas. Particularly difficult was how these childhood experiences affected your moods, behaviors, and relationships. After careful assessment, these sessions were conducted in the manner customary for the treatment of Post Traumatic Stress Disorder (through the use of Cognitive Behavior Therapy and psychoeducation, utilizing a strengths-based perspective and trauma informed care in talk therapy). Treatment terminated when you stated you felt you were managing well and wished to discontinue. My recommendation is that you return to treatment if you experience an increase in symptoms, continue to utilize the strategies we discussed, and maintain overall wellness.

Thank you for trusting me with your care.

Best Regards,

LICSW

I continue to learn new ways to cope.

Somehow, all of my experiences have prepared me for this moment and that is to take care of my wife. Beth has taken care of me all twenty-seven years of our marriage and she has prepared me well to handle taking care of her. It is true that what doesn't kill you makes you stronger. Although my wife is doing great, the threat of MS is always there.

Of all the experiences that I have survived, I must say that being positive, hopeful, and having basic good health saved my life, over and over again. I am counting on that principle to keep my wife strong. Whatever your experiences are I encourage you to write your own story and create your own set of values.

I constantly work on my set of values and I feel that everyone should have a set of values that are written.

These values can drive who you are. With a set of values, you can be counted on and folks around you can rely on you for certain characteristics in any given situation.

Below are the ten behaviors that have helped me live a blessed life:

1. Be honest with yourself.
2. Be your own hero but follow great leaders.
3. If you get sick, it helps if you are healthy.
4. Trust no one 100 percent unless it is earned over time.
5. Find ways to exercise.
6. Be spiritual even if you are not religious.
7. Stand on your own two feet but seek professional help when you are suffering in silence.
8. Select friends carefully and cultivate everlasting relationships.
9. Look for ways to help others on a daily basis.
10. Work hard to master your emotions.

To say that martial arts had an impact on my life is an understatement. At the moment I met Master Kim, I was absolutely broke with absolutely no dreams, no hopes, and no real future. Master Kim is an author of many books and CDs but my favorite quote from him that inspires me is woven into the fabric of my leadership style. Thank you, Sir!

"A leader's nature is to follow the truth, to inspire willingness in spirit, to make sacrifices, and to stand by justice. He must treat each and every human being with equal respect, empathizing with their sadness, joy, hunger, and triumphs. He must listen to the opinions of all, yet make competent decisions himself, remaining independently able to withstand moments of solitude." - Grand Master Y. K. Kim

Final Thought

"Big boys don't cry, but grown men do"
Robert Butler 2015
Thank you, brother!

What are your thoughts, experiences, or feelings about any topic of this book? My email is kickman45@yahoo.com

To share your story of Domestic Violence, visit my blog at http://domesticviolencehelp.tips

Please share this link with someone you know that might be ready to express their story.

About the Author

Ken Butler

An accomplished martial artist, graphic artist, poet, personal trainer, and registered clergy with experience related to the topic of domestic violence. He is well-respected among his peers for his tenacity to survive anything that comes his way including serious medical conditions, family tragedies, depression, PTSD, auto accidents, and more. He is the recipient of multiple community service awards for outstanding services to several communities from RI to Florida. He is recognized as a leader in the wellness industry and has won awards that celebrate his leadership and team building capacities. Being the eighth sibling of ten children that was raised by a single mom only ignited his passion for creativity and determination that is truly remarkable. He often says, "Be your own hero." He certainly is considered a hero by so many individuals from all walks of life that he impacted through his inspiring relationships, teachings, and insights.

CPSIA information can be obtained
at www.ICGtesting.com
Printed in the USA
BVOW05s0822130617

486766BV00017B/70/P

9 781683 481515